MAGNIFICENT ME!

Written by Randa Canter

Illustrated by Rebecca Tibbetts

To El, Teag, and Mae—the three of you are incredible examples to me of resilience and pure love. This rollercoaster we call life is more full, fun, and wonderful because of you. Your sacrifices are noticed, and your service is appreciated more than you could ever know. You are each magnificent to me. I love you!

–RC

To my wonderful husband, Brent, for his support. Also, to Scott and Nathan for their faith in me and constant encouragement when I wanted to quit.

– RT

LAWLEY
PUBLISHING

This edition first published in 2022
by Lawley Publishing,
a division of Lawley Enterprises LLC.

Text Copyright © 2022 by Randa Canter
Illustration Copyright © 2022 by Rebecca Tibbetts
All Rights Reserved

Lawley Publishing
70 S. Val Vista Dr. #A3 #188
Gilbert, AZ 85296
www.LawleyPublishing.com

Hello, my name is Macie Jo.
I have some essential things to share.

Tips and tricks I'm learning
that I find are quite rare.

I'll teach you by telling stories
about my brother Parker and me.
Listen closely, and you'll realize
how magnificent YOU can be!

Sometimes in life,
there are heartaches,
sad and stressful
times, it's true.

The tough stuff can seem really big.
You may think you don't know what to do.

You get tired like you're jumping hurdles,
leaping over them, WAY off the ground.
It's hard and can make you feel heavy,
so unhappy you just want to frown.

If you search, you'll see positive things.
They're not always easy to find.

Spot them, and your life will change,
bringing tremendous peace of mind.

When you notice glad things in your life,
you'll start to see them more and more.
And the feelings you have will be great,
happiness to the very core.

Like eating the best piece of cake;
delicious, yummy, and OH SO sweet.

It creates a satisfying warmth,
a feeling that just can't be beat!

So, jump the hurdles. They don't leave,
but are easier to overcome.
Put your focus on the cake in life
and enjoying every last crumb!

I'm a fantastic big sister
to a determined younger bro.
I love him from the TOP of my head
down to my little pinkie toe.

Parker was born so tiny and cute.
There's no way I could be more proud.

I smile when he makes
cooing noises
and help my mom
when he screams LOUD!

Sometimes I see Mom and Dad cry too.
Do you remember the hurdle thing?
Our newborn Parker has special needs,
and they don't know what that might mean.

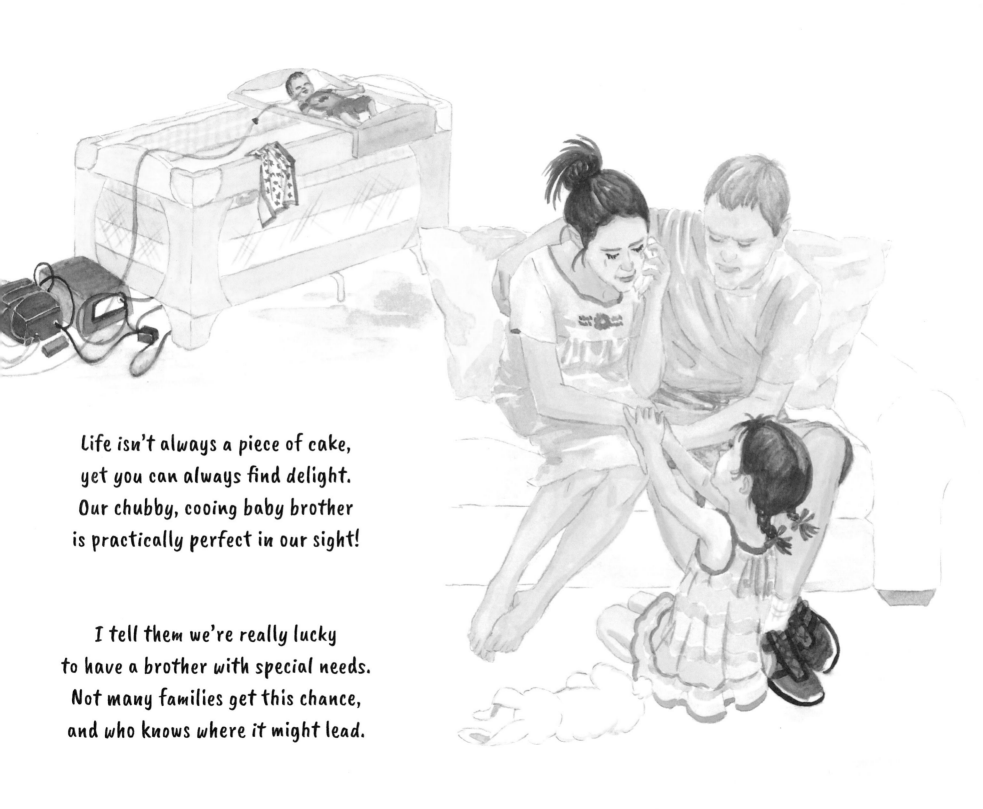

Life isn't always a piece of cake,
yet you can always find delight.
Our chubby, cooing baby brother
is practically perfect in our sight!

I tell them we're really lucky
to have a brother with special needs.
Not many families get this chance,
and who knows where it might lead.

Hospital stays happen quite often.
I stay back with Grandma and Gramp.

We make get-well cards,
crafts, and forts.
Then pretend we're sleeping at camp!

I worry if Parker's okay
and wonder when he will be home.
When I'm unhappy
and miss him and Mom,
I video-call them on the phone.

This helps me, but sometimes I fret
and have moments I feel all alone.
I kneel down to pray. Peace comes.
God's love is so clearly shown.

Dad takes me to his hospital room.
Volunteers bring us neat toys—
two books, meant for Parker and me,
for being a good girl and boy.

What's the hurdle?

**What's the
piece of cake?**

We are home now, all together!
I'm relieved Parker is okay.
We settle back into home life.
I prefer these quiet kinds of days.
The sun is out. It's oh so hot.
I can't wait to jump in for a swim,
But Parker has a spica cast
to help straighten his lower limbs.

An umbrella and fan by his chair keep him comfortable, shaded, and cool.
His cast stays on for twelve HOT weeks, but that can't keep me out of the pool!

I do flips and huge cannonballs
to help him enjoy the pool too.
I'm good at creating and thinking
of entertaining things to do.

What's the hurdle?

What's the piece of cake?

Being part of a family is an adventure all the time.
Parker is growing and learning, and right beside him, SO AM I!
I'd rather be playing at the park. Therapy can seem like a drag.
There's time for both, though, and I've found, in each, there is good to be had!

We work closely in his therapy,
exercising while playing games.
My example helps him try hard,
so someday he can do the same.

What's the hurdle?

What's the
piece of cake?

I notice differences in my life between most of my friends and me.
Their families move so fast to get to the places they want to be.

Not us. We move very slowly, at an unhurried turtle pace.
We have lots to unload and prepare before we head out on OUR race.

There are some benefits, though, like front row parking at events.
We don't have to walk very far, so our energy is rarely spent.

What's the hurdle?

What's the
piece of cake?

We go to extra appointments,
so Parker can have his check-ups.
While we patiently wait, it can be boring,
especially listening to the grown-ups.

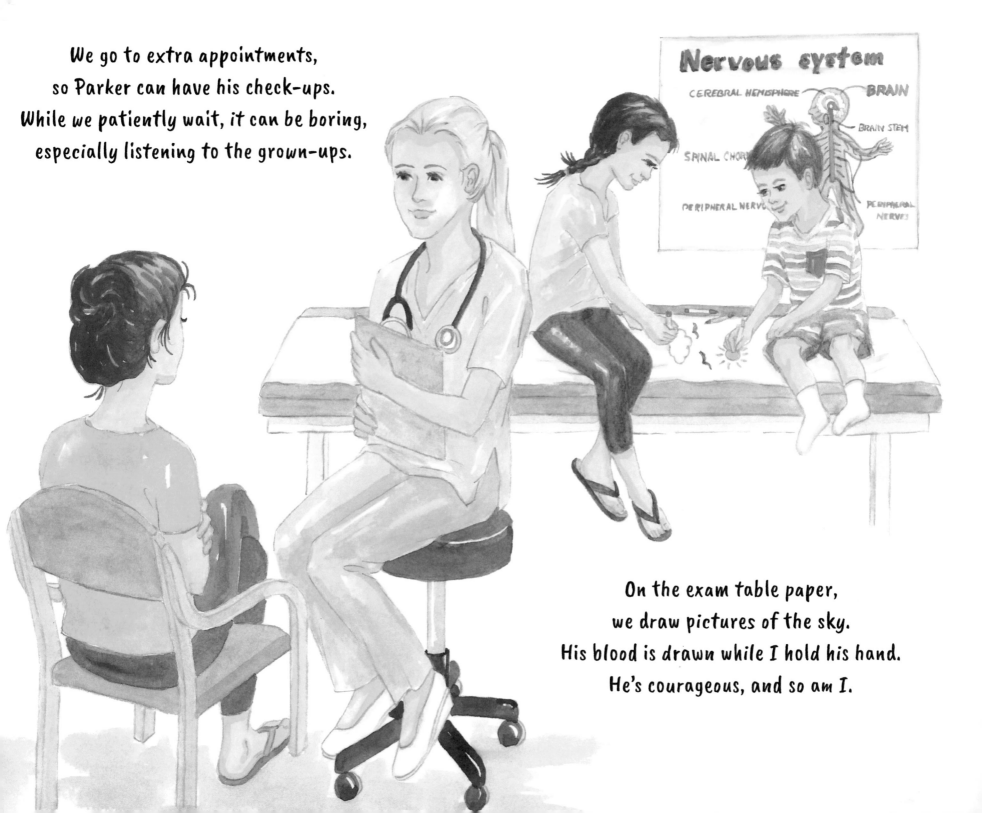

On the exam table paper,
we draw pictures of the sky.
His blood is drawn while I hold his hand.
He's courageous, and so am I.

It's sad to watch as he gets poked,
but these tests keep him healthy and strong.
So, I'll be brave and support him
each time I get to come along.

What's the hurdle?

What's the
piece of cake?

Our family enjoys sporting events.
So, imagine our smiles to the brim—
when Parker sticks out at the football game,
making the star player approach him!

Next, we ALL get to meet the head coach,
receive jerseys, and have a VIP tour.
We join the team at the last big game,
storming the field through the tunnel door!

It's things like this that remind me
how each of our lives lifts the other.
I bless him, and he blesses me
by being my AWESOME kid-brother!

What's the hurdle?

What's the
piece of cake?

When Parker gets ready for surgery,
he can't eat or drink for eight hours.

I hide to eat, so he doesn't see,
I'm doing ALL that's in my power.

The surgery he needs is outpatient, which means he'll come home right after.
We'll eat popsicles, snuggle, then joke, and share some much-needed laughter.
He brings me home a soft teddybear instead of choosing one for him.
Seeing him smile, sharing the surprise made MY face and heart make a big grin!

What's the hurdle?

What's the
piece of cake?

There aren't many places that work
for wheelchair users to play team sports.
The long drive to the baseball field
for HIS dream to happen seems short.

I volunteer as his "Buddy."
Helping him out is so much fun!
When Parker makes it all the way home,
I cheer loudest for his HOME RUN!

He's one of MY biggest cheerleaders.
His love means more than he'll ever know.
He supports me at my recitals
and at home as I practice cello.

What's the hurdle?

What's the
piece of cake?

I try not to be a bother.
Speaking up can be hard to do,
When Parker requires extra attention,
but I need Mom and Dad's help too.

It's important, so I share my feelings
even when it seems really scary.
All children have unique needs
that parents work to carry.

They understand and hold me tight,
we talk, and they are my guides.
Together we find the positive,
deciding we're on the perfect ride!

We remind each other we're lucky
to have a brother with special needs.
Not many families get this chance,
and who knows where it might lead.

What's the hurdle?

What's the piece of cake?

Homelife is full of daily tasks.
We make dinner, do homework, and clean.
Parker's body requires other jobs,
important things that need done in-between.
Together we do many of our chores.
He dries dishes and hands them to me.
Parker can't reach up high — but I can.
We make a strong team — GUARANTEED!

I get asked to pitch in
more than preferred.
I'd choose to relax
in my bed and read.
But I'm growing more
aware each day,
which allows me to
notice those in need.

What's the hurdle?

What's the
piece of cake?

At the playground, I see a girl,
frightened, in her seat, all alone.
I walk right up and approach her,
saying, "Hi," in a soft, tender tone.

The girl doesn't respond with her voice,
but her smile shows up loud and clear!
We play and laugh together.
Our joy is beyond compare!

I try to find a way we're the same
when someone is different than me.
It's a pretty simple thing to do.
Being nice is the BEST way to be!

What's the hurdle?

What's the piece of cake?

There are moments I feel tearful
and wish Parker could run and be free.
But my choice to be resilient
is shaping MAGNIFICENT ME!

I love being Parker's big sister.
I teach him to share and be kind.
And when he becomes a big brother,
I'm confident he'll do just fine.

I know you've got hurdles in your life.
They'll never be too big for you.
Keep jumping over and around them.
Find the cake that is waiting for you!

It's there to be found, I promise.
And will bring a joy you can't outgrow.

YOU'RE
MAGNIFICENT
just as you are.

Choose to let your
loving-kindness show!

Note to Parents & Caregivers:

Anyone who has a sibling knows that there is give and take in the sibling relationship. Each member added to a family requires additional splitting of resources and time. However, family life is an environment for crucial and invaluable education that cannot be received anywhere else. If the "typical" sibling relationship has its highs and lows, then it's no surprise that having a sibling with "special" needs is viewed by many as a challenge. My hope for this text is to bring awareness to both adults that interact with and children who face these unique life circumstances. Let conversations flow and be open to hearing the joy and sorrows of these incredible siblings. You have the opportunity to guide siblings and help them form special bonds with each of their family members. I pray that you take this responsibility seriously and don't allow any child to ever be left behind as "the other one."

WHAT YOU SAY AND DO MATTERS!

ALWAYS:

- Recognize and praise the kindness, service, and sacrifice of siblings.
- Listen—Be a safe place where siblings can freely share their feelings and concerns.
- Pause—Life is busy, but every child matters! Spend individual time with siblings. They need your time too!
- Inform—Knowledge is power! Children are often left in the dark about their sibling's diagnosis, prognosis, and medical care despite having a lifelong need for information.
- Share age-appropriate information, asking for help from Child Life Specialists and other providers. Written material can help increase understanding and comprehension.
- Acknowledge that a situation is sometimes hard as an adult too. This reflects reality and opens lines of communication.
- Keep a sibling's "special" needs an open discussion topic.
- Get involved—Many organizations exist with the specific focus of bringing hope and help to families, including siblings of children with special medical needs. Ask your child's hospital case manager, your pediatrician, and state or local organizations for your child's specific diagnosis (i.e., Spina Bifida Association of Arizona) for referrals. You can also google: HopeKids, Sibshops, Beads of Courage, Dream Factory, and Make-a-Wish, just to name a few

NEVER:

- Assume a child heard or understands what is happening with their sibling. Be bold and ask!
- Shame a child for their feelings—it's normal at times to feel a wide range of ambivalent feelings as a sibling.
- Take for granted the unique role siblings play in each other's lives. ALL siblings impact one another in a multitude of ways.
- Forget that we are all unique individuals. Remember, every child has an identity separate from being the sibling of their brother or sister who lives with a disability.
- Be afraid to offer a compliment. Kind words go a long way!
- Let the opportunity to share your love and concern pass. We all could use a lot more love!

OTHER BOOKS BY AUTHOR RANDA CANTER

UNIQUELY YOU!

When friends Parker and Crew recognize all the ways they are different and the same as each other, their lives become full of new and exciting adventures! Join them on their journey of showing how to be Uniquely You!

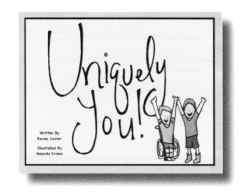

I AM SAFE

Being the boss of your brain is hard work. But you don't have to suffer from paralyzing fear. You can choose to feel happy and safe! "I Am Safe" will arm you with courage to believe the mantra:
I AM PREPARED AND KNOW WHAT TO DO.
I AM THE BOSS OF MY BRAIN.
I HAVE THE POWER TO FEEL SAFE.

"I Am Safe" is a brilliant book that teaches children how to understand and manage big emotions by empowering them to transform their dark thoughts into light thoughts. Randa Canter skillfully guides children to a state of internal safety with simple and reassuring language. The inspiring statement, "I am the boss of my brain," is a message both young and old can embrace.

Marianne Turley, MC, LMFT
Licensed Marriage and Family Therapist

MEET THE AUTHOR

Raised in a family of six, Randa Canter has shared the ups and downs of the sibling experience. She's also learned to juggle the weight of a blended family with five children, including Parker, who was born with Spina Bifida. After Parker's birth, Randa sought any information related to his diagnosis and how best to raise her family in these unique circumstances.

One evening, as she sat crying to her husband, their oldest daughter, Ellie, knelt in front of them and said, *"I think we're lucky to have a brother with special needs because not many families get this chance."* Those wise words left a lasting impact on the entire family and inspired *Magnificent Me!*

With Ellie now away at college, Randa and Mike stay busy with Teagan, Macie, Parker, and Millie, at their home in Gilbert, Arizona, where you might find Randa playing pickleball or standing on her head—two of her favorite things!

MEET THE ILLUSTRATOR

Rebecca Tibbetts received her Associate of Arts degree from Mesa Community College and her Bachelor of Fine Arts degree from Arizona State University.

She currently resides in Mesa, Arizona, with her husband and teaches Art at Heritage Academy-Mesa. She has four grown children and eight grandchildren.

"Illustrating children's books has been one of my dreams for many years, but I have never done it until now. I am grateful to Lawley Publishing and to Randa for giving me this opportunity to illustrate *Magnificent Me!*"

MEET THE SIBLINGS BEHIND THE INSPIRATION

Although *Magnificent Me!* appears to only show the sibling relationship between Macie and Parker, it is a compilation of actual situations experienced collectively by Ellie, Teagan, and Macie over the years as older siblings to Parker. All three of these outstanding individuals have shown maturity, tolerance, and patience in their roles as advocates and examples to their younger siblings, especially in gracefully handling the ups and downs of a disability in family life. They continue to amaze me in their ability to exemplify a love and understanding that is beyond their years.

Lightning Source UK Ltd.
Milton Keynes UK
UKRC031008050422
401126UK00001B/10

9 781956 357134